The Pen-pal from
Outer Space

First published in Great Britain 1998 by Mammoth
an imprint of Reed International Books Limited.
Michelin House, 81 Fulham Rd, London SW3 6RB
Published in hardback by Heinemann Educational Publishers,
a division of Reed Educational and Professional Publishing Limited
by arrangement with Reed International Books Limited.
Text copyright © Franzeska G. Ewart 1998
Illustrations copyright © Simone Lia 1998
The Author and Illustrator have asserted their moral rights
Paperback ISBN 0 7497 3432 9
Hardback ISBN 0 434 80313 8
10 9 8 7 6 5 4 3 2 1
A CIP catalogue record for this title is available from the British Library
Printed at Oriental Press Limited, Dubai

Franzeska G. Ewart

The Pen-pal from
Outer Space

Illustrated by SIMONE LIA

 **YELLOW BANANAS**

To my mother, Kate Ewart

Chapter One

IF THERE WAS one thing in the whole wide world that was the *worst* thing in the whole wide world it was being at a new school, Jasbir thought for the millionth time.

It wasn't that people didn't try. Mrs Hyslop, the teacher, tried very hard to make Jasbir feel welcome. On Jasbir's first day, Mrs Hyslop introduced her to all the other children and asked for a volunteer to look after her.

1

Mrs Hyslop chose Shahid. Shahid took his job very seriously and Jasbir listened politely as he gave her three conducted tours of the playground.

'Did you know,' he said as they walked, 'that some frogs lay their eggs on the female's back and the skin grows over them and then when the tadpoles hatch they have to eat their way out?'

Jasbir admitted that she had not known.

'And did you know that some spiders actually live underwater?' Shahid went on. 'They construct special webs, and trap enough air in them to enable them to live for many days. And talking about spiders, it is said that a spider can live for a year – yes, a year – without any food at all. Did you know that?'

By the end of the day Jasbir felt rather dizzy – partly because she had walked in circles and partly because she had shaken her head so much.

On the second morning, Mrs Hyslop chose the MacKenzie twins, Rory and Gordon.

'We're identical . . . ' Rory said.

' . . . but I'm three minutes older,' Gordon finished.

'And we have a grandmother in Glenrothes,' Rory told her.

'And another grandmother in Dundee,' Gordon added.

'We also have a grandfather in Leicester,'
Rory said.

'But he is not the husband of our
Glenrothes granny . . .' Gordon pointed out.

'. . . or our Dundee granny,' Rory said.

'It's a tad confusing,' they both admitted,
shaking their identical heads gravely.

On the third morning, Mrs Hyslop forgot to choose a person to look after Jasbir. Jasbir was secretly very relieved.

She *had* rather hoped that perhaps Mrs Hyslop would ask Aneesa. Aneesa sat right at the back of the class and was very quiet. Jasbir had never actually *spoken* to Aneesa, but she had seen her in the cloakroom on the first morning when she was looking for a place to hang her coat. Aneesa had given her such a lovely smile that Jasbir knew she was nice.

It had been a lovely rosy smile, but it had also been very shy. Since then, whenever they met, Aneesa seemed as though she would speak, and often Jasbir opened her mouth to say 'Hi' but somehow nothing happened. It was very sad.

One day Mrs Hyslop held up a large piece of paper.

'Primary Four,' she said, 'I have a surprise for you. I have got a list of pen-pals – from all over the world. Now listen carefully, and you can each choose one to write back to.'

There was silence as everyone listened carefully.

Jasbir nearly put her hand up for Tanya from America because she had a horse and wanted to be Miss America when she grew up, but then she changed her mind.

Then she nearly went for Hiroko from Japan, but decided against it when she heard she kept crickets as pets.

'Right – last one,' Mrs Hyslop said suddenly. 'This is Franz from Germany. It says, "I study English since two years now and I seek much practice. I love difficult sums."

So – who is going to take Franz?'

Jasbir's heart sank. She wished she had chosen Hiroko, despite the crickets. She put up her hand. Then she heard Mrs Hyslop say, 'Fine, James – I am sure you will give Franz lots of very good practice. You'll have to remember your full stops and capitals though, and learn your four times table.'

Jasbir looked round to see James taking a note of Franz's name, and then she looked back at Mrs Hyslop.

'Oh, Jasbir,' Mrs Hyslop gasped, 'I am sorry! I haven't got a pen-pal for you! It's with you being new. I'll get you one, of course, but it will take a few weeks – sorry. Would you like to read a book for now?'

So Jasbir went to the library corner while everyone else began their letters. She chose a book but she didn't feel like reading. She tried to comfort herself with the thought that she would get a pen-pal eventually, but it didn't help.

After break, as she trailed sadly back to the library corner, Jasbir noticed a piece of paper lying on her desk. She picked it up.

No one was watching her, so she sat down to read it. As she read, her mouth opened wider and wider and her heart beat faster and faster.

Jasbir *did* have a pen-pal. A very strange pen-pal indeed.

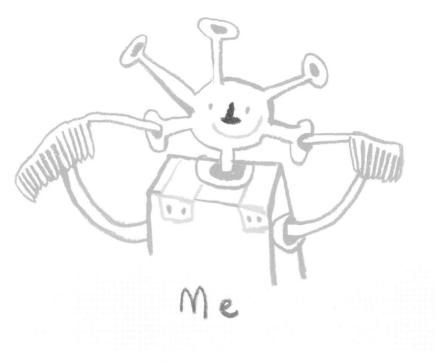

Me

Chapter Two

JASBIR STARED AT her letter. At the top was a strange drawing. It looked a bit like a robot, with sucker-like things growing out of its head and two thin arms with lots of spindly fingers.

Under the drawing was written one word – 'me'.

Jasbir took a deep breath and began to read.

Dear Jasbir,

Greetings from Planet Zargos!
I am your new pen-pal and
my name is ZipPy* (watch the way you
write it — we Zargons don't just keep
capitals for the beginnings of words!).
I just happened to have my Intergalactic Tracer Screen
set to Planet Earth and I picked up your brain waves
—we Zargons are incredibly good at that. I realised
that you were sad because you didn't get a pen-pal.
So here I am—your very own pen-pal— and I hope
we will be friends! See my portrait at the top of
the letter? I'm doing the Zargon greeting, which
we always do when we
meet someone we really
like. I have a
little bother.
Here he is:
You'll notice that he

hasn't got as many fingers as I have.
That's because we Zargons grow more and more
fingers the older we get. There are some very old
Zargons who have over fifty fingers on each hand.
It makes us terribly
good at sums.
Are you good at sums?
I also have a pet,
and this is it:

We call it Blippo and
we control it from a box.
Please write back. Leave your letter on the
third shelf of the teacher's cupboard, beside the
chalk, and I will cause it to rematerialise
on Zargos. As we say in Zargon — be
happy, and may everyone you meet make you
want to stick your fingers in your ears.

ZipPy*

Jasbir folded up ZipPy*'s letter and put it in her bag. She knew exactly what she would do. Maths had been the biggest nightmare since she joined the new school. Somehow, she just couldn't get the hang of it and maths tests were the worst. Jasbir pictured ZipPy* with all his fingers, and she smiled.

She would ask ZipPy* to use his superior powers to help her with the maths test.

When the bell rang, Jasbir was the first out of the classroom. She ran home, shut herself in her bedroom and slowly, carefully, she began to write:

Dear ZipPy*,

I am very happy to have you as my pen-pal.

I will tell you all about myself, but first there

is a little matter of a maths test I would like

to discuss. . .

14

Chapter Three

IT WAS INCREDIBLY dusty on the third shelf
beside the chalk.

Jasbir waited till everyone had gone out,
then headed for the teacher's cupboard with
her letter.

She had spent a long time the night before
composing it. She had told ZipPy* all about
her family – she too had a little 'bother' and
she had tried hard to draw Pritpal so that
ZipPy* should really know what he looked
like.

At the end of the letter, just in case ZipPy*
might forget, Jasbir had written:

P.S. Please don't forget about the maths test.

I would be most grateful for any help at all - I am

hopeless at maths, probably because I've only got

ten fingers.

For the rest of the morning Jasbir could
concentrate on nothing. Her eyes kept going
to the cupboard as though she expected to
see her letter floating
out and up to the planet
Zargos, but nothing
happened.

After lunch it was time for the maths test – and still nothing. Jasbir put her hand up.

'Mrs Hyslop,' she said, and Mrs Hyslop looked at her in surprise.

'Can I get some more chalk for you? There's none left.'

Mrs Hyslop looked rather puzzled. 'Isn't there?' she said. 'Oh very well, thank you, Jasbir.'

Jasbir rushed to the cupboard. She felt along the third shelf . . . and, yes! There *was* a reply! Her own letter had gone, and in its place there was just one very small piece of paper.

Jasbir took out two long pieces of blue chalk and

the paper and hurried back to her seat.

'Right, Jasbir – are you ready?' Mrs Hyslop said, and Jasbir nodded.

'Good,' Mrs Hyslop sighed. 'Now – I have six teams of boys, and there are four boys in each team, how many boys is that altogether?'

Jasbir felt the usual sickening feeling in her stomach. Carefully, so no one would see, she uncrumpled the piece of paper from Planet Zargos. It said:

Of course I will help you with your maths test – nothing simpler! Just remember – altogether means add or multiply. That's important. The other important thing is – keep calm, and I will be with you.

Be happy, and M. E. Y. M. M. Y. W. T. S. Y. F. I. Y. E.

Jasbir looked at her test paper. Suddenly she remembered ZipPy* with all his funny fingers and she felt a warm rosy feeling of calmness she had never felt before – particularly not in a maths test.

Mrs Hyslop repeated the first sum. As she did, something seemed to click inside Jasbir's head.

'Altogether,' she thought. 'That means add or multiply – nothing simpler!'

And, slowly and carefully, Jasbir wrote her answer – 24 boys.

So it went on. Jasbir felt so calm and happy knowing ZipPy* was there that the answers seemed to come as easily as could be, and when the papers were marked, Jasbir scored twelve out of twenty.

It wasn't the most brilliant score in the class – but it was better than Jasbir had ever scored in her life.

But the best thing was knowing that, if you had a friend to teach you the rules and keep you nice and calm, maths tests could get better and better.

Chapter Four

AFTER SCHOOL, MRS Hyslop asked Jasbir to
stay behind.

'What an improvement in your maths,
Jasbir,' she said. 'You deserve a gold star! Oh
dear me,' she went on, 'why does this drawer
get into such a mess? Ah! Here it is,' she said
at last, fishing a pastille tin out from under a
mass of rubber bands and confiscated toys.

She opened it and sighed.

'None left! My, what a good class I have –
they go through gold stars so quickly. Run

and get me another packet out of the cupboard please, Jasbir.'

The stars were on the second shelf, but as Jasbir was used to looking on the third shelf beside the chalk she checked there too.

And to her utter amazement, she saw a new letter! She gave the stars to Mrs Hyslop and then she rushed home to read it.

Dear Jasbir,

Thank you so much for your letter. I loved hearing about your family. Today I am going to tell you about an adventure I once had. One day I was taking my pet Blippo for a walk when I heard a noise coming from the top of an Ognam tree. When I looked up, all I saw were five terrible red eyes staring back at me.

As soon as I saw the eyes, I knew I was looking at a

terrible two-mouthed purple Hooley! Hooleys can freeze you into ice, you know, and lick you with their two awful tongues until in the end . . . you disappear!

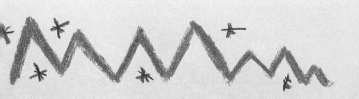

'Hoooo! Hoooo! Hoooo!' it went.

Then it stopped.

I waited and waited, but nothing happened. At last I could not bear it any longer. I had to move. I looked up at the Hooley, and do you know what it was doing, Jasbir? It was laughing! And then I saw why. It was watching Blippo, and Blippo was turning somersaults faster and **faster.**

Now, I don't know if I explained but Blippo, my pet, is not actually alive. If you saw Blippo's inside, he's

just wires and fuses and little lights and switches.

That means that, although he has got feelings of a

sort, he doesn't really belong to anyone. So I took

a big deep breath and,

in as brave

a voice as

I could manage

I said to the Hooley,

'You can have Blippo if you like him, Mr Hooley.'

The Hooley gave one enormous

'Hooo!' reached

down and lifted Blippo ever so

gently into the Ognam

tree and off it went.

I hope you like my adventure story and I am
really looking forward to hearing yours.
  Write soon. Be happy, and may
everyone you meet make you want to
  stick your fingers in your ears,

ZipPy*
X X X X X

Chapter Five

JASBIR SAT ON her bed and thought.
Compared to ZipPy*'s wonderful adventure
with the Hooley, nothing that had happened
to her seemed remotely interesting. What
could she write? She wasn't good at stories at
the best of times.

At school the next morning, Mrs Hyslop
said, 'Do you remember how the little boy in
your reading book loved to listen to his
grandpa's stories? Well, this morning you are

going to write your own story, like Grandpa's. Make it as exciting as you can.'

So Jasbir sat, as she had the night before, and thought and thought about what she could write. She was staring at the blank sheet of paper when suddenly a strange thing happened.

Just like the day before in the maths test, Jasbir felt a warm, rosy glow inside and she pictured ZipPy*'s face looking at her across space. And she knew that there was someone who really wanted to hear about her adventures.

Happily, Jasbir began to write:

My Adventure with Green Paint

Once upon a time when I was about four and a half we lived in a house near Manchester.

It was a new house, and the houses next door were not even finished.

One day I took my little brother, Pritpal, to see them. Pritpal was only two.

Outside the houses we found some tins of paint. It was green paint that the workmen were using to paint the doors. They had left the lid off one of the tins.

They had also left their brushes.

I took a brush and I dipped it in the paint. Then I painted big strokes of green on the wall. It looked lovely! Then Pritpal wanted a paintbrush too. I gave him one and dipped it in the green paint for him.

Well, I was only four and a half – and after all the workmen should never have left the paint tin with its lid off.

Then . . . I decided to paint Pritpal.

At first he thought it was funny. Then he began to cry, so I took him home.

He was so sticky, I made him walk. I didn't fancy carrying him. Then the worst thing of all happened.

Pritpal was screaming so hard, Mum heard

him and came running out of the house.

She was wearing a beautiful pale pink cardigan that my auntie had just knitted for her. It was all covered in little sequins, and it had taken my auntie months to knit.

Mum was so upset to see Pritpal crying, she held out her arms and said, 'There, there, Pritpal sweetie – whatever has happened to you?'

And Pritpal threw himself into Mum's arms and rubbed his face all over her beautiful pale pink cardigan . . .

When Mum got over the shock of seeing Pritpal covered in green paint, she was very angry with me!

Pritpal and I had to be scrubbed and scrubbed, and I had to have my hair washed with turpentine. And the beautiful pale pink cardigan with the sequins . . .  had to be thrown in the bin!

Mrs Hyslop read the story. 'This is wonderful, Jasbir!' she said. 'It's worth at least three gold stars.'

She let Jasbir stay in at break to copy the story out – and when she wasn't looking, Jasbir slipped the first copy triumphantly onto the third shelf of the cupboard.

Chapter Six

FOR THE NEXT few weeks Jasbir and ZipPy*
went on exchanging letters till Jasbir felt that
she knew almost all there was to know about
him. But as the summer holidays got nearer
Jasbir began to feel very sad. How could she
send letters to ZipPy* if she couldn't put them
on the third shelf of the cupboard?

Then an idea came to her and she wrote to
ZipPy*.

Dear ZipPy*,

Thank you for your last letter. 'Zango'
sounds a marvellous game. I will suggest it to
Mrs Hyslop next time we are at the gym.

ZipPy*, I am going to ask you for a big favour,
and I hope you won't mind. You know how one
of your superior powers is reading brain waves?
Well, I was wondering whether
you could perhaps get inside
the brain waves of a
girl in my class. Her name is Aneesa. I would
just love to be her friend, you see.

I mean, it's great
having you, and I hope we'll

be pen-pals for ever and ever, but it's a long summer without the teacher's cupboard, and it would be so nice to have an Earth friend to really do things with.
Could you manage to get inside Aneesa's head and tell her that I think she's the nicest person in the class and I want to be her friend?
Please write soon.
Be happy, and may everyone you meet make you want to stick your fingers in your ears.

Jasbir

Chapter Seven

THE NEXT DAY at school, Jasbir kept looking at Aneesa to see if ZipPy* had contacted her, but Aneesa just got on with her work as usual.

However, in the afternoon two very odd things happened that made Jasbir feel puzzled. Slowly she began to realise that everything was not as it seemed.

The first was during Spelling. Jasbir heard Mrs Hyslop talking to Aneesa.

'Now really, Aneesa – I don't expect such

carelessness from you! Look at the way you have spelt "brother" – you have missed out the "r" not once but every time. Now, rub out each "bother" and write it properly – BROTHER.'

Jasbir sucked the end of her pencil and frowned. ZipPy* always spelt 'brother' as 'bother'. Jasbir had thought it was a Zargon joke.

After playtime, a second odd
thing happened. Jasbir
heard Mrs Hyslop talking
angrily to Aneesa.

'Oh, Aneesa – what a
terrible mess all over
your work! It's covered
in blue chalky fingerprints! What have you
been up to, Aneesa?'

Spelling 'brother' as 'bother'? Jasbir thought.
Covered in blue chalkdust? There was
something very fishy going on – but surely
not? Surely not Aneesa, of all people?

Jasbir tiptoed to the cupboard and reached
up to the third shelf for the message she
knew would be there.

It was written on a very small piece of
paper, and it said:

Meet me behind the bike shed after school,

ZipPy*

When the bell rang, Jasbir rushed out. As she ran to the bicycle shed, there was a tiny part of her that did expect to see ZipPy* standing there. But another part of her knew that ZipPy* would not be there, and that in fact, ZipPy* would never write to her again.

And of course she was right. For, standing behind the bicycle shed was someone who, in the end, would be an even better friend than ZipPy* had been.

Jasbir stopped running. Aneesa turned to face her and began to walk slowly towards her, a large smile spreading across her face.

Then, at just the same time, both girls stopped and smiled at one another as they stuck their fingers in their ears and they both stood together in the rosy pinkness of Planet Zargos.

Yellow Bananas are bright, funny, brilliantly imaginative stories written by some of today's top writers. All the books are beautifully illustrated in full colour.

So if you've enjoyed this story, why not pick another one from the bunch?

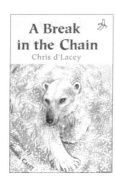